# SCOOBY-DOO!
## An Early Reading Adventure

# MONSTER IN THE WOODS

By Michelle H. Nagler
Illustrated by Duendes del Sur

**ABDOPUBLISHING.COM**

Reinforced library bound edition published in 2017 by Spotlight, a division of ABDO. PO Box 398166, Minneapolis, Minnesota 55439. Spotlight produces high-quality reinforced library bound editions for schools and libraries. Published by agreement with Warner Bros. Entertainment Inc.

Printed in the United States of America, North Mankato, Minnesota.
042016     092016

THIS BOOK CONTAINS
RECYCLED MATERIALS

**PUBLISHER'S CATALOGING IN PUBLICATION DATA**
Names: Nagler, Michelle H., author. | Duendes del Sur, illustrator.
Title: Scooby-Doo and the monster in the woods / by Michelle H. Nagler ; illustrated by Duendes del Sur.
Description: Minneapolis, MN : Spotlight, [2017] | Series: Scooby-Doo early reading adventures
Summary: Scooby and the gang are on vacation at the lake. But a big, hairy monster seems to be lurking around their cabin. Is he after their Scooby-Snacks? It's a case only the Mystery Inc. gang can solve!
Identifiers: LCCN 2016930649 | ISBN 9781614794684 (lib. bdg.)
Subjects:  LCSH:  Scooby-Doo (Fictitious character)--Juvenile fiction. | Dogs--Juvenile fiction. | Vacation--Juvenile fiction. | Monsters--Juvenile fiction. | Mystery and detective stories--Juvenile fiction. | Adventure and adventurers--Juvenile fiction.
Classification: DDC [Fic]--dc23
LC record available at http://lccn.loc.gov/2016930649

**Spotlight**
A Division of ABDO
abdopublishing.com

Scooby and the gang were on
a vacation.
They were all excited to see
where they were staying—a
brand new log cabin on the
lakeshore.
"Let's unpack the van and head
to the lake," said Fred.

Fred and Daphne went to unload
the van.

Velma helped Shaggy and Scooby
in the kitchen.

"Like, I'm starved, Scoob," Shaggy
said. "Let's unpack the food."

"Rokay!" Scooby said.

They were gobbling down snacks
when Shaggy suddenly heard
a noise.

"What was that?" asked Shaggy.

"Probably just some other
campers in the woods," said
Velma.

Scooby and Shaggy decided to kick back in the lake with some inner tubes.

Fred, Daphne and Velma tried to catch some fish.

"I got one!" yelled Velma.

"What a great vacation, Scoob," said Shaggy.

Scooby heard a sound behind him and out of the corner of his eye, he thought he saw a monster!

But when Shaggy looked around, there was nothing there but a little fish on the end of Velma's line.

Back at the cabin, Scooby acted out what he had seen: a big, hairy monster with very sharp claws.

Fred and Daphne looked outside, but they didn't see anything.

"It must have been a bear," said Velma.

"I believe you old buddy. There's a monster out there," said Shaggy.

"Shaggy, will you and Scooby
go get some wood for the fire?"
asked Velma.

"Rokay!" barked Scooby.

"Like, did you forget about the
monster?" asked Shaggy.

"Would you do it for two
Scooby-Snacks?" asked Daphne.

"Rokay!" said Scooby.

Scooby and Shaggy went into the forest.

Scooby found some sticks.

"Great job, Scoob!" said Shaggy. "Let's bring these back to the cabin."

Then Scooby found some bones.

"Yikes!" said Shaggy. "I hope the monster didn't leave these. Let's get out of here!"

They were on their way back
to the cabin when Scooby
stumbled into an enormous
footprint.

"Like, these footprints are too
big for a bear," said Shaggy.

"Rig," agreed Scooby.

"Run!" Shaggy said.

Scooby and Shaggy led their
friends back to the large footprints.
"These footprints are very big,"
Velma said, studying them.
"And these bones are unusual
too," said Daphne.
"Looks like we've got a mystery
to solve!" said Fred. "Let's look for
clues."
Velma, Fred and Daphne searched
the woods for clues.
Scooby and Shaggy went to look
around the lake.

The first thing Scooby and Shaggy found was a picnic table full of food.

"This is where we saw the monster," Shaggy said to Scooby. "The monster must like fried chicken and french fries, just like us!"

Suddenly, the monster came
charging toward them.
Scooby hid under the table.
"We're sorry...we didn't mean to
eat your food," said Shaggy.
But right behind the monster
was a man holding a
video camera.
"Cut!" yelled the man.

Fred, Daphne and Velma came running.

"What happened?" asked Fred.

"We're making a movie about Bigfoot," said the man.

"That explains the giant footprints," said Velma.

"And the bones," said Daphne.

"What about the chicken?" asked Shaggy.

The man in the Bigfoot costume took off his mask and sat down.

"I love fried chicken," he said. "Say, do you know anyone who wants to be in a movie?"

Scooby barked, "Scooby-Dooby-Doo!"

# The End